Print information available on the last page

Rev. date: 07/14/2015

To order additional copies of this book, contact:
Xlibris
1-800-455-039
www.xlibris.com.au
Orders@Xlibris.com.au

For my family.

Ahwen's journal.

Written & illustrated by Alice Alder

Ahwen was a little fox who loved exploring. He would wander through forests and fields in search of new and exciting adventures.

Valley Notes;

five trees past Charwood's home ⚹

Turn at tail ⚹

⚹ Farm gate is always open after Sun set!

Best place to find food!!

Charwood's Valley

Stem rose

good for eating.

4

Whenever he found himself on an adventure Ahwen would write, draw and paint as he went along. His journal was full of secret fox maps and letters from his dear friends. Ahwen kept his most important memories in his book.

But, the day Ahwen lost his journal was the most memorable of all! He didn't know where he had lost it or when. Ahwen began frantically searching for his book. He searched high and low. He searched in logs and deep down in rabbit roles, but he could not find his beloved journal.

"How will I remember all my adventures and special memories if I don't have my book?", thought Ahwen.

He didn't waste anytime!
Ahwen ran as fast as his little
paws could carry him. Over
hills, under logs and through
the valley he ventured.
Ahwen was on his way to
see Harn.

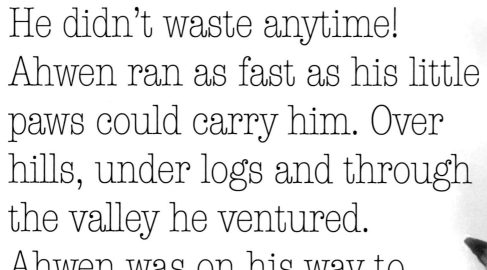

9

10

When he arrived, Harn was busy shooing
blue birds off his antlers.

"HARN! Have you seen my journal!?",
puffed Ahwen.

Harn looked down at Ahwen and smiled.
"Good morning my dear fellow.
What's this about your journal?".

Ahwen explained that he had lost his book.

"I'm sorry, I haven't seen your little book around the valley. But, maybe Charwood has seen it down one of his many burrows".

"Yes! That's a great idea", said Ahwen. "I was in the hills the other day. I have to find my journal Harn. If I don't I will never see my memories again".

And with that he kicked up his heels and ran up the valley towards the hills. But, Ahwen was running so fast he didn't see Charwood and crashed into him!

"My word! Where are you off to in such a hurry?", asked Charwood, as he brushed dirt off his ears.

16

"Sorry. Have you seen my journal?",
asked Ahwen.

"If I don't find it I will never see my
memories again", he sobbed. A single
tear rolled down his cheek and fell to the
ground.

Charwood put his paw on his friends shoulder and said,

"You will always have your memories even if you don't have your journal. When something is important and special you remember it, always. Fox's have very good memories and they never forget".

20

Ahwen smiled from ear to ear. "You're right! I *can* remember everything that was in my journal. I *can* remember who my friends and where they live. I remember all the names of the plants in the valley. And I *can* even remember where *all* the paths are that I take on my adventures!" Ahwen laughed. "Foxes really do remember everything".

And even though Ahwen never found his journal he now knew he would never lose his memories. He would always have them safe in his heart and in his thoughts.

But, if you are ever in the forest , near the hills, and you find an old, dirty journal hold onto it. Keep it very safe. Enjoy the stories.

You might have just found Ahwen's journal.

Printed in the United States
By Bookmasters